While we're waiting for the bus,
My baby brother makes a fuss,
But all the grannies look at him and smile.

They "Ooh" and "Aaah" and "Coochy-coo"
And "Tickle-tickle! Peek-a-boo!
He's the bonniest baby in Dundee!"

The Fourth Bonniest Baby in Dundee

Michelle Sloan & Kasia Matyjaszek

Picture Kelpies

Then one day I see a sign.
A contest *here*! A search to find:
Who's the bonniest baby in Dundee?

"No time to lose!" I shout to Mum.
"There's a trophy to be won!
Let's get our baby home and in the bath!"

"What will he wear, though?" I complain.
"All his clothes have mucky stains!"
I search through vests and tops and dungarees

We wash and brush and smooth his hair,
And find a sailor suit to wear.
He's off to win this contest – just you wait!

On the bus, the grannies smile
And mutter, "What a bonnie child!
That bairn's the winning baby of Dundee."

And as he's bounced from knee to knee,
I close my eyes and start to dream –
Our baby makes the front-page headline news!

But then there's an almighty shudder –
A sway, a lurch, a clunk, a judder.
Jeezy peeps, the bus has broken down!

We all pile off and stand around.
We're stranded at the edge of town!
And next it starts to bucket down with rain...

No time to wait, we have to run –
The baby judging has begun!
I'm sure that we can make it if we try.

Down Perth Road we make a dash,
Through soaking streets we sprint and splash.
We've got to get a wriggle on – let's go!

We're almost there! But as we stand
To wait and wait for the green man,
Our bus shoots past and everybody waves.

The pavement's packed; it's just too busy –
So many folk out in the city –
Till I yell, "Bonnie baby coming through!"

EXPLORE DUNDEE

We make it in the nick of time,
And join the other bairns in line.
Och no! Our bonnie baby's in a state!

He's sticky, claggie, clarty, blue,
With oily clothes, all dripping through.
We've brought the dirtiest baby in Dundee!

The lady judge walks down the line.
She's coming closer all the time.
We try to clean him up but make it worse!

She looks at him and says, "Oh my!"
He blows a raspberry in her eye!
We've brought the rudest baby in Dundee!

The judge looks shocked; her face is grim.
She shakes her head. We'll never win!
Our baby starts to chuckle to himself.

And then the judge begins to smile.

A laugh escapes, and in a while
She's yowling, snorting,
whooping with delight!

At last she says, "Your bairn's a joy –
A giggling, cheeky, fun wee boy.
That makes him rather bonnie in my book."

He didn't get the winning prize,
But he's a champion in our eyes.
The fourth bonniest baby in Dundee!